Rai

Written by Lynne Benton

Illustrated by Tony Morris

For Mary

Chapter 1

I am running, faster and faster. My feet skim over the rough grass. My heart is pounding, and I am terrified, but I dare not stop. I have to warn them.

I sat up, shaking all over. I could feel the sweat trickling down my back. I had never been so frightened.

Who, or what, had I been running from? And who did I have to warn? It had been so real. Was that really me who had been running away? Me, Jack Watson, aged nine-and-a-half? What had happened?

It was half-term and we were staying in this cottage – me, my sister Lucy, Mum and Bob. It would have been okay, if it hadn't been for Bob.

Bob was Mum's boyfriend. I couldn't stand him. Dad left us years ago, when Lucy was a baby, and we've never seen him since. Lucy and I can hardly remember him now, so we were quite happy, just the three of us. Until Bob came along, that was.

At first we didn't mind him too much, but it wasn't long before he was spending all his spare time with us. That was when I started hating him. He wasn't nasty to us. He was just always there, sitting on our settee, eating our food and watching our telly. We never had Mum to ourselves any more.

So when Mum told us Bob's old uncle had just died and left him a cottage in the country, I thought he might go and live in it and leave us in peace.

But Mum said, 'Bob wants us to go down and see the cottage and stay there for a few days.'

'But it's half-term!' I said, horrified. 'I want to do things here with my friends. I don't want to go to some boring cottage with HIM!'

'Sorry,' said Mum, 'but I've said we're going.'

'This is going to be the most boring half-term ever!' I grumbled.

I couldn't have been more wrong.

The cottage was okay, but the garden was really good. It was big and wild with plenty of trees to climb.

'What a great garden!' said Lucy.

'It's all right,' I muttered.

'Bet I can climb higher in those trees than you,' said Lucy.

She was always trying to outdo me, probably to make up for being younger. But I couldn't be bothered to prove it now. I went indoors and Lucy followed.

'Where's the telly?' I asked Mum.

'Oh, there isn't one,' she said.

'No telly!' I exploded.

'But we'll miss our favourite programmes!' said Lucy.

'Uncle Alf didn't like television,' said Bob. 'But I'm sure you'll find other things to do.'

'It's not fair,' I grumbled.

Then we went up to our bedroom.

'Bunks!' I said in disgust. 'You mean we've got to share bunks?'

'I don't mind,' said Lucy.

'Well I'm going to have the top one!' I said.

'No, I want it!' said Lucy.

'I'm the oldest!'

'You're a bully!' shouted Lucy.

We ran downstairs to ask Mum.

'Why don't you toss for it?' said Bob. So we did, and Lucy won.

'That's your fault!' I shouted at Bob. 'It's not fair!'

Angrily, I slammed the door and ran back up to the bedroom. I grabbed my football and kicked it hard against the wall, wishing the wall was Bob. The ball rebounded across the room and shot under the bottom bunk. CLUNK!

I went cold. What had I broken? Mum would be furious! I bent down to see what I'd hit. It seemed to be a bundle of brown canvas and metal poles. I pulled it out. Whatever it was, it didn't look broken.

'Mum!' I called. She came in with Bob. 'Look what I've found!' I said.

'Good heavens, it's the old tent!' said Bob. 'Fancy it still being here! I slept in that once, years ago.'

I stared at him for a moment. Then I had my great idea.

'If I let Lucy have the top bunk, can I sleep in the tent in the garden?'

Mum looked at Bob. I held my breath. He nodded and Mum smiled.

'I'll put it up for you after supper,' said Bob.

'Thanks,' I muttered. So he should, I told myself.

After we'd eaten, we found a good place for the tent on the grass, behind the cottage, and in no time Bob had fitted it all together.

'There you are,' he said, hammering the last peg into the ground.

I was just thinking maybe he wasn't so bad after all, when he spoilt it by saying, 'There's just one thing I should warn you…'

'It's fine!' I snapped. I didn't want a lecture. So I dived inside the tent, pulled the flap across, and lay down. I heard him walk away, and sighed with relief.

It was great to be on my own at last. No Bob to annoy me, no Lucy to argue with. From now on, the tent was my territory. I lay down and grinned to myself.

And that was when it happened.

Can you think of five reasons why Jack was in such a bad mood?

Chapter 2

Afterwards I sat there for a bit, while my breath returned to normal, going over it again in my mind. The running, the terror, were still so real, but I supposed it must have been some sort of dream. What else could it have been?

Cautiously I opened the tent flap. Everything seemed normal out there. The light was on in the kitchen, and the radio was playing.

I went indoors to get my night things and a torch. If it happened again, I wanted to be prepared.

'Everything all right?' asked Mum.

'Yes, thanks,' I said. Bob looked at me, but didn't say anything, so I got what I needed and hurried back to the tent.

At first I was almost scared to lie down again, but after a while I must have dozed off.

There's a strange, thick, smoky
smell. I open my eyes. I am lying in a
wooden hut. It's quite dark, but there's
a fire burning in the middle of the
floor. A woman in a long blue dress
is bending over it. She hasn't noticed
me. I seem to be wearing a rough,
scratchy brown tunic. I am covered
by some sort of animal skin, which is
warm, but smells funny. I turn over
and suddenly I see two bright eyes
staring at me, a face framed by
matted dark hair. For a moment I
think it's Lucy. Then I realize it's not.
This is a girl I've never seen before.

The eyes blink and a voice
hisses, 'Edric! Are you awake?'

She is talking to me. She speaks again. 'Edric! Wake up!'

I try to speak, but nothing happens. I try to sit up, but I can't.

Then the woman straightens up and looks across at us.

'If you two are awake, you can go out and see if the men are back from hunting yet.'

Then the girl who looks like Lucy but isn't, sits up and pokes me.

'Come on, Edric!' she says. 'Let's go and find Father! Let's see if they've caught a wild boar! And don't forget to bring your wooden swallow. You know that it's brought you good luck ever since Father made it for you.'

I don't know what she is talking about. Then I am aware of something hard sticking into my belt. I pull it out. It is a small wooden object in the shape of a bird. It is beautiful and I can see from its forked tail that it is a carved swallow.

The smoke from the fire grows thicker, and I start to cough...

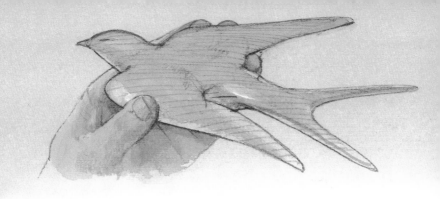

And then I found myself back in the tent. The air was clear, there was no smell of smoke, and I was alone. No girl poking me, no woman, no fire and no wooden swallow.

My heart was thumping. What had happened?

I picked up my torch, switched it on and flashed it round the tent. There was nothing to see. I switched it off and lay down again, thinking. It didn't seem to make any sense. Where had I been? Who were those people? And who was Edric, and why did they all think I was him? Even more odd, why did *I* think I was him? But before I could puzzle it out, I'd fallen asleep.

Next morning, in the daylight,
I decided it must have been a dream.
I would put it out of my mind.

That day Mum said we were
going sightseeing.

'Bob says the area is of great
historical interest,' said Mum.

'History!' I said in disgust. 'But
we're on half-term!'

Mum took no notice and it
didn't stop Bob going on about
the Anglo-Saxons who used to live
there. He said the cottage was on the
site of some old Anglo-Saxon
settlement.

'History is school!' I grumbled.
'I'm not interested!'

Mum looked grim. 'If I have *any*
more rudeness from you, Jack, there'll
be no more tent in the garden!'

I couldn't risk that.

'Sorry,' I said.

So we went round some castle and
Bob told us all about it. I didn't listen.

I couldn't help thinking about the girl in the hut, and the man who had made the wooden swallow for me. I wondered what would happen when I went in the tent that night.

Mum sounded surprised when I volunteered to go to bed early.

'Are you feeling all right, Jack?' she asked.

'Just tired,' I said, practising a yawn. 'It's been a busy day.'

What did Jack learn about how the people lived, when he went back in time?

Chapter 3

The girl is here again. I know now she is my sister, Elfreda. We are in a forest, collecting wood. Suddenly she laughs and picks up a long stick.

'Bet I can beat you in a fight!'

I grin, and pick up a stick too. 'Bet you can't!' I say, and we pretend to fight like warriors.

Elfreda is very good at it, but at last I manage to disarm her.

'It's not fair,' she says. 'You're stronger than me! Anyway, come on. Mother will be waiting for the firewood. She is cooking for the feast tonight.'

Suddenly I hear something rustling in the bushes, not far off.

'Hush!' I whisper. 'What's that?'

Elfreda looks at me, her eyes sparkling with excitement. 'It might be a wild boar!'

The rustling comes again.

'It sounds bigger than a boar.'

'You're just scared,' Elfreda jeers.

I shiver and touch my wooden swallow for luck. Perhaps it will protect me from the thing in the bushes. Then I have a disturbing thought.

'It might be a wolf!' I say.

Elfreda shivers too.

Hurriedly we pick up our bundles of wood and run back to the village. As soon as we are inside the boundary fence, Elfreda pulls the gate fast shut behind us.

'Now the wolves can't get us!' she says.

Wolves! I thought when I woke up.
Maybe that was what I'd been running
from, that first time. I wished I
understood it all.

That day Mum, Bob, Lucy and I
went to the river, not far from the
cottage, and had a picnic.

Lucy and I went to play hide and
seek in a wood nearby. I soon got
bored and started thinking about
Elfreda. Suddenly I heard a rustling
in the bushes behind me. I whipped
round, my heart in my mouth.
Wolves!

And then something
sprang out behind
me. I felt two paws
on my shoulders.
I jumped in
terror, and
let out a
shriek.

'BOO!'
cried Lucy.

I shook with rage.

'You idiot!' I yelled. 'You frightened the life out of me!'

'I was only playing, Jack,' she said. 'You went all white, but you knew it was me…didn't you?'

I opened my mouth and then shut it again. How could I tell her I'd thought she was a wolf?

'Course I did.' But I was still shaking inside.

We went back to the riverbank where Mum and Bob were sitting.

'What was all the shouting about?' asked Mum.

'We were just playing,' I said. But I was still angry with Lucy for frightening me. Elfreda would never have done such a thing, I thought, for all her teasing. She took wolves seriously. I wondered if she had heard them again.

Why do you think Jack was so frightened when Lucy jumped out at him?

Chapter 4

'It's not fair!' Elfreda grumbles. 'Why won't you take me fishing, Father?'

Father grins. 'Fishing is men's work, Elfreda. You must stay at home with Mother and help cook the feast.'

Elfreda scowls. 'I don't want to cook,' she says. 'I want to go fishing like you and Edric. I want to learn to fight, too. I wish I were a boy.'

'I pity anyone who has to fight with you,' grins Father. 'I'm afraid I'm only taking Edric today.'

I smile at him. He is a kind man, and I am proud that for the first time I am allowed to go fishing with him and the other men.

'Today is a great day,' says father. 'It is Alfwold the Thane's birthday, and as he is the most important man in the village, tonight there will be a big feast in the Great Hall. That's why we need to catch plenty of fish.'

'Father,' I say. 'We heard something in the forest this morning. Elfreda thought it might be a wild boar.'

'I wanted to catch it for the feast,' says Elfreda, 'but Edric said it might be wolves, so we came home instead.'

Father nods.

'Very sensible,' he says. 'No one has seen any wolves round here lately, but it's as well to be careful. Now, off you go and help your mother, Elfreda. Edric and I have work to do.'

Father collects the nets and we take them down to the river. The others are there, waiting for us.

Father shows me how to hold the net and trail it under the water.

It is harder work than I expected, and I get very tired, but by the time we have finished I have caught several fish all by myself.

Then, just as we are collecting up the fish, I hear a rustle in the bushes nearby.

'Father! Listen! It's that noise again!' I hiss, grabbing his arm.

But Father hasn't heard it. It is quiet again now. I strain my ears, but I can't hear a sound.

Father pats me on the shoulder.

'You're hearing things, Edric!' he says. 'Nobody's seen any wolves round here for years!'

I touch my wooden swallow for luck. I am sure I heard something.

When I woke up, I felt exhausted, as if I'd been working hard all night. But I'd only been asleep, hadn't I? I hadn't really been catching fish in the river...

Mum noticed, of course.

'What's the matter, Jack?' she asked. 'You look worn out!'

'Perhaps it's the tent?' suggested Bob. 'I remember when I –'

'Of course it's not the tent!' I said, angrily.

I argued and got cross with Mum, Bob and Lucy all day. In the end Mum said she was glad it was bedtime and told me to go out to the tent so they could all get a bit of peace.

I didn't need to be told twice.

What do you think Bob was going to say about the tent before he was interrupted?

Chapter 5

I am in the Great Hall. There is a fire in the middle and people sitting at tables all round the edges. Elfreda and I are on long benches at the side. Everyone is drinking out of horns and eating meat, fish, bread and vegetables.

But just then we hear all the dogs start barking outside. Someone near the door goes out to see what has set them off and comes back a moment later, followed by a stranger. The stranger is dressed like everyone else, in tunic and leggings, but his are torn and dirty and he looks very tired.

'I have travelled a long way,' he says, 'and I bring news.'

Alfwold raises his cup. 'You look tired and hungry, friend,' he says. 'Won't you join us in our feast? When you have eaten, you can tell us your news.'

The stranger sits down and Elfreda and I watch him. He drinks a cup of mead straight down and eats every last scrap of his meal.

The stranger stands up.

'My friends,' he says, 'I must thank you for your kindness, but I bring you bad news. There are raiders in these parts.'

There is a buzz of consternation at this news. Everybody has heard of the raiders – huge bearded warriors from over the sea. Some people call them Sea Wolves because, like wolves, they are said to be fierce raiders, merciless to any who stand in their way.

'There have been two raids near here in the last month.'

Alfwold frowns. 'This news has not reached us,' he says. 'But don't they come looking for gold and jewels? We have no jewels so why should they bother us?'

'My village had no jewels either,' says the stranger. 'It was just like yours. But they have discovered our land is good for farming. They want to steal it and settle here.'

I am suddenly very afraid.

'What about the people who live there?' I ask.

The stranger looks grim. 'They kill them, boy. They search the village, take anything valuable, and kill all the villagers. I was lucky. I escaped.'

I shiver. Elfreda shivers too. Everyone is silent.

'They took us by surprise,' the man goes on. 'But at present they send only one ship at a time, so if you are prepared, you may defeat them.'

Alfwold stands up. 'Thank you for your warning, friend,' he says. 'May we offer you shelter for the night?'

The stranger shakes his head. 'No, thank you,' he says. 'I must go on and warn the people in the next village.' And he bows and leaves.

'We'll be all right, won't we?' whispers Elfreda. 'Father will fight them off. We can help him!'

I wonder if Elfreda has any idea how fierce the raiders are. 'Of course,' I say. I hope I'm right. Then I remember the rustling in the bushes. Was it a wolf, or could it have been a Sea Wolf, looking for a good place to raid...?

I woke up suddenly, my mouth dry with terror. Now I knew what it meant. I knew the connection. The raiders were coming. They were the enemy I'd been fleeing from. I had to warn the village. There was no time to lose.

I shut my eyes and desperately willed myself back there. But it was no good. Nothing happened. When I opened my eyes, I was still in the tent. I tried and tried, but still nothing happened.

And at last I realized I couldn't get back till night time. I would just have to wait.

I went indoors for breakfast.

'Feeling better today, I hope?' asked Mum.

'Yes thanks,' I said. I couldn't explain. Nobody would believe me.

It was a strange sort of day. The weather was hot and heavy, as if it was waiting too.

'I think we'll have a thunderstorm before bedtime,' said Mum. We spent the day at the wildlife park, which should have been good, but I just couldn't concentrate. I was too worried and too tired and too hot.

Then, just as we were having our supper, we heard the first rumble of distant thunder. Mum shivered.

'You'd better stay indoors tonight, Jack.'

I stared at her in horror. I couldn't stay indoors, not tonight. I had to get back to the tent and back to my other life.

'I don't mind thunder,' I said.

'No,' said Mum.

'But, Mum!' I said, desperately.

'I've said no, and I mean no!'

Do you think Jack will be able to warn the villagers in time?

Chapter 6

I lay tense in the bottom bunk, listening to the thunder rumbling away in the distance.

I tossed and turned, wondering what would happen if the raiders came and I wasn't there to warn the villagers. They needed me, I knew they did.

Soon I heard Lucy snoring above me, so I knew she was asleep. Later, I heard Mum and Bob turning the lights out and going to bed. At last, there was silence.

I've got to go out to the tent, I thought. I can't let the raiders get them.

Carefully I slid out of bed, opened the door, and crept down the stairs. The front door was locked and bolted, and it was hard to pull the bolts back quietly, but I managed it.

The air was stifling. There was no wind and as I hurried towards the tent I saw a flash of lightning light up the sky. I counted the seconds. Sixteen before the next rumble of thunder – four miles away. Too far to worry about. I had more important things on my mind.

As soon as I was inside the tent, I lay down and closed my eyes.

It is cool, dark and silent. No birds are singing. It is early dawn and I am on my way to the riverbank looking for firewood.

I should have collected it yesterday, but I forgot. When I reach the high ground, overlooking the river, I look down.

Then I freeze.

A long, narrow boat, with a dragon's head at the front, is gliding silently along. There are round metal things hanging over the sides, and I realize they are shields. The oars dip in and out of the water without a sound. My mouth goes dry. I am almost too terrified to move, but some instinct warns me to drop to my stomach, out of sight. I crawl to the edge and watch.

They stop rowing, and the boat pulls up by the bank. It is full of huge men, with long fair hair underneath iron helmets.

Raiders!

They are quiet, intent and menacing. I have never seen so many men make so little noise.

With hardly a sound, they spill out of the boat, lifting off their round shields to take with them. They are all carrying axes and swords. They look like giants. Then they begin to creep purposefully towards the village. My village, where Father and Mother and Elfreda are asleep.

And I remember what the stranger told us about the terrible things the raiders had done in his village. I am horribly afraid.

I reach for my wooden swallow. I need it now, to bring me luck. It is not there.

I must have forgotten to pick it up. It must be in the hut. I try not to think of this as an ill omen.

Trying desperately to keep out of sight, I wriggle backwards until I cannot see the raiders any more. Then I leap to my feet and start to run, faster than I have ever run in my life. My feet skim over the rough grass.

My heart is pounding, and I am terrified, but I dare not stop. I have to warn them. Only when I reach the fence do I dare to look over my shoulder. The raiders are not in sight yet, but I know they cannot be far behind. I run inside and bar the gate. Then I race to the nearest hut and bang on the door.

'Raiders!' I shout. 'Help! Raiders! Help!'

I don't wait for an answer, but run to the next hut.

'Raiders!'

I can hear people stirring behind me as I race through the village. I cannot stop until I have warned Father.

Suddenly I hear a loud splintering noise behind me, as the raiders attack the gate with their axes. Then they surge into the village, with terrible, bloodcurdling cries.

As I reach our hut, the door opens, and Father comes out, brandishing his sword.

'Well done, Edric,' he cries. 'We're ready for them!'

Then I realize everyone is awake. There is a lot of shouting and the clash of swords and spears. We Anglo-Saxons may not be as big as them, but we are fierce when we're threatened. We won't give in without a fight.

'Look after your mother and sister, Edric,' calls Father, as he charges into the battle.

The noise is deafening now. I turn and see the other women and children huddled at the fence, away from the fighting.

Mother and Elfreda are in the hut. Mother is looking desperately worried, but Elfreda's eyes are sparkling with excitement.

'I want to join in!' she says.

'Oh, Elfreda!' I say, exasperated, as I hurry them out of the hut.

Then Elfreda sees what is happening, and hears all the shouting and the fearful clashing of weapons.

She picks up a stout stick and as we reach the others she says bravely, 'Don't worry about us, Edric. I'll look after Mother and the other children.' And I know she won't give in without a fight, either.

Then I smell something, and whirl round. Someone has set light to the Great Hall. Above the noise of battle I can hear a fierce crackling, as smoke and flames leap into the sky. The air is thick with the smell of smoke. Some of the other huts are on fire, too.

'I must go and help Father!' I cry, and hurry off to find him.

There are men fighting everywhere, but I can't see Father. Then a huge hand is clamped over my mouth. I struggle and find myself in the grip of an enormous raider. He is incredibly strong and I am paralysed with terror. I cannot even scream.

And suddenly, Father is here. His sword is battered and has smears of blood on it. I have never seen him look so fierce.

'Leave my son alone!' he bellows, charging at the man.

With a roar, the raider pushes me aside and turns to Father. He has a heavy axe in his hand. He whirls it round his head. The axe cuts the sword in two, as if it was no more than a twig. Father is left holding the stump as the Viking lifts his axe again.

'Father!' I scream. 'Look out!'

Father dodges as the axe falls where his head would have been. But the axe has caught his shoulder, and I see blood spurt out from the deep wound. His arm dangles, useless.

I must help him. What can I do?

Then I remember my lucky swallow, still in the hut. It is my last hope. But as I turn, I see our roof is now alight. I must hurry.

I dive in, snatch up my swallow from the bench, when I see the raider raise his axe again.

I am so angry I don't stop to think.

I stand in the doorway and fling the wooden swallow at him with all my might. To my great satisfaction, it hits him on the forehead. Startled, he staggers back and drops the axe. Father grabs it.

'Well done, Edric!' he says, glancing over his shoulder at me. Then his eyes widen with horror.

'The roof!' he cries. 'Look out!'

But before I can move, everything goes black.

What do you think will happen to the village?

Chapter 7

The air was still thick with smoke when I came to, and it was very hot. I was coughing. My head hurt. I was afraid to open my eyes.

Someone was carrying me. Was it the raider? Or had Father rescued me after all?

I opened my eyes. There were flames all around me. For a moment I thought the whole village was on fire. And suddenly I realized I was back in my own time, and it wasn't Father or the raider carrying me. It was Bob.

Then I heard the loud siren of the fire engine and soon the garden was full of men and women with hoses, spraying everything in sight and calling to each other. What was going on? One of them took me from Bob and carried me indoors.

'Jack! Are you all right?' cried Mum, tearfully.

'He'll be fine, thanks to your husband,' said a fireman. 'The tent's gone, though, and that big beech tree in the garden. But luckily we've stopped the fire getting to the house.'

At that moment Bob came in. He was wearing his pyjamas, which were torn and scorched. His face was dusty and there seemed to be something wrong with his hands.

Then I passed out again.

When I opened my eyes, the fire-fighters had gone, and a strange man was there, bandaging Bob's hands. He turned to me.

'Ah, you're awake,' he smiled. 'I'm Doctor Smith. How are you feeling?'

'Sore,' I said. 'And my head hurts. But I think I'm all right.'

'You're lucky,' he said. 'Your dad got you out of the tent just in time. If it wasn't for him you'd have been burnt to a crisp. We're taking you both into hospital overnight.'

I looked across at Bob, sitting in the chair with his bandaged hands and his face grey. I wondered what to say. 'Thank you' seemed too little for what he'd done.

Then Lucy came downstairs, rubbing her eyes.

'What's happened?' she asked, looking with interest at my wounded head and Bob's poor hands.

Mum picked her up and cuddled her.

'How did you manage to sleep through all that thunder?' said Mum. 'A bolt of lightning hit one of the trees in the garden, and it caught fire and fell on the tent. Bob went out to rescue Jack. He just got him out in time.'

'It's not fair!' grumbled Lucy. 'I miss all the exciting things!'

'Sorry,' said Bob.

I looked at him, curiously.

'How did you know I was in the tent?' I asked.

Bob shrugged.

'I knew you wanted to go out,' he said. 'And when we heard the crash, I wondered if you'd slipped out after we'd gone to bed. So I looked in your room.' He smiled, weakly.

Suddenly I felt ashamed. It was my fault Bob had been injured. I shouldn't have been out there.

He had put himself in danger, just to save me. Like Edric's father did, to save Edric. I remembered then that everybody had thought Bob was my father. At that moment, I wished he was.

They sent us home from hospital the next morning, though we were both still feeling fragile. Mum fussed around and made us both comfortable in the sitting room. Then she took Lucy off to get some food, leaving Bob and me together.

I felt awkward, but it had to be said.

'I'm sorry, Bob,' I mumbled. 'I didn't mean you to get hurt.'

Bob smiled. 'I'm sure you didn't,' he said. Then he added, 'Can you tell me why were you so very keen to go out to the tent last night? In spite of the thunder?'

I hesitated. Then I told him everything, all about Edric and Elfreda and their father, and the raiders.

He didn't interrupt. But when I'd finished he said, 'Ah...Now I understand. Yes, it all makes sense.'

'Does it?' I was surprised. 'I wish it made sense to me.'

So he told me.

When he was twelve, he'd stayed in the cottage with his cousins, Guy and Allie, and they'd put the tent up in the garden. Allie, who was about Lucy's age, had insisted on trying it first. But she soon came indoors, shaking, and said she never wanted to go in a tent again.

'Of course, we laughed at her. We thought she'd been scared of a few creepy-crawlies, so Guy and I said we weren't scared, we'd try it.'

I gazed at him. 'What happened?'

Bob smiled.

'Nothing – only we both woke
up with terrible headaches, so we
didn't bother with the tent again.
We just rolled it up and put it away.
I'd forgotten all about it until you
found it. But now you've told me
what happened, I'm sure it's the
same tent.'

'Did Allie ever tell you what had frightened her?' I asked.

'No, never.'

'So what do you think it was?' I asked.

Bob looked thoughtful. 'I think you were both caught in a time-slip,' he said. 'Something about that tent in this garden must have caused you both to go back to the time of the Viking raids. There were several around here in the ninth century, and I think I told you this cottage was built on an old Anglo-Saxon settlement.'

Of course he had. And I'd been too much of an idiot to listen.

'If Allie went back in time like you did,' said Bob, 'back to the night of the raid, no wonder she was frightened!'

'But I don't understand why *you* didn't go back,' I said.

'Guy and I were too old. I think Edric needed someone his own age to live his story. Perhaps he couldn't finish the job. If the Vikings caught him before he could get back to the village, he would need to find someone else to warn them. He needed you.'

It was a weird thought.

'I wish we could find out what happened afterwards,' I said. 'I want to know whether they all survived. But I suppose it's too long ago.'

Bob thought for a moment. Then he said, 'Uncle Alf was very interested in local history. He might have some books about it. Let's go and look in his study.'

We found several but only one that gave much detail about Anglo-Saxon times. I started reading.

'Listen to this,' I said suddenly …
"The village was attacked by Viking raiders in 875, but it is thought that someone raised the alarm, as the villagers fought off the Vikings. After that they lived in peace for many years."

'So Edric did save the village,
after all!'

'Or *you* did,' said Bob.

What would have happened, I
wondered, if I hadn't gone back in
time?

I looked at Bob. Why had I ever hated him? Not only had he saved my life, he had believed my strange story. And managed to explain it.

But all I could say was, 'Edric forgot his lucky swallow. That's why he needed me.'

Now Bob is talking about going to live in the cottage all the time, and he's suggested to Mum that we all go and live there too.

And you know, now I've got used to the idea, I don't think I'd mind. We get on okay these days, Bob and me. Besides, he's the only other person I can talk to about what happened. I never told Mum, or Lucy. After all, how could I expect them to believe me?

He says if we all go, he could have another bedroom built on for me and I could have my own bed – so no more bunks for Lucy and me to fight over.

And of course, he says, we would get a television.

I'm beginning to think having a father wouldn't be so bad after all.

Why did Bob believe Jack's story?

How did Jack feel about Bob at the beginning of the story? Did he change his mind?